James Brunton Stephens

Convict Once

A Poem

James Brunton Stephens

Convict Once
A Poem

ISBN/EAN: 9783337397685

Printed in Europe, USA, Canada, Australia, Japan

Cover: Foto ©Andreas Hilbeck / pixelio.de

More available books at **www.hansebooks.com**

BY

J. BRUNTON STEPHENS

𝔏𝔬𝔫𝔡𝔬𝔫

MACMILLAN AND CO.

1871

CONTENTS.

PROËM.

I, HYACINTH, of whom she wrote, now write :

    Not from the hope of fame, or wish for praise;

    But that, in waning of her latter days,

She willed her warning tale should see the light

And whispered with her fading breath that I

    Should soften nothing that she did reveal,

    But charter her confession with a seal

Of manual pardon—as I do hereby.

And ere ye scorn her troubles, passion-fed,
   Her wilful choosing of the crooked path,
   And ere ye make a virtue of your wrath,
I pray you all, remember—she is dead.

Forgive the passions that she could not curb,
   The heaving trouble of a fevered breast.
   She's very quiet now.   She hath her rest:
And there is none can wake her, none disturb.

I, who have most to pardon, pardon all,
   As I myself beseech forgiving grace;
   And live in hope that I shall see her face,
Even as an angel's, at the Judgment call.

PART FIRST.

! CONVICT ONCE.

I.

FREE again! Free again! Glory and brightness
 of Life's Saturnalia!
What is denied me now? What is withheld me
 now? I who am free!
Surely the Sun holdeth revel! and Jubilee reigns in
 Australia!
And there are echoes of joy in mine ears from far
 lands o'er the sea.

* * * * * *

2

Wrought even to pain with emotions long-prisoned and
    ardours volcanic,
  Great with the promise of things that have grown
      in the silence of years,
Seems to me now that my soul should be mother of
    issue Titanic.
  Drunken with Freedom I leap, as a maddened steed
      plunges and rears.

3

Seven retributive years have not left my tried spirit
      unshaken,
  Vulture-like tearing me; harpy-like soiling me,
      blinding my eyes.
Yet from the depths I emerge; like a giant refreshed
    I awaken,
  Strong for the purpose of life, for the struggle, the
      victory, the prize.

4

Ah ! I must calm me, nor triumph too soon with

exultant delirium :

Silence, and patience, and foresight, to these is

the victory given :

Life's raging sea is not cloven at the sound of the

timbrel of Miriam ;

But at the touch of the rod of the SEER the dark

waters are riven.

5

Yes, I must calm me, remembering that Freedom

restores me to Duty—

Not to the license and rapture of such as have

struggled and won.

Passion hath proved itself fatal, and fatal the magic

of beauty ;

I must try wisdom and prudence, contented to

walk ere I run.

6

Have I not found what I longed for? Already my
star is propitious.
Heaven hath found me a home where life's sweetest
amenities smile ;
Lowly indeed, but unmerited, poor to a spirit
ambitious ;
Yet a sweet oasis-fountain whereat I may linger
awhile.

7

Here I behold it, my long-cherished dream of a
home in the wild wood :
Here I shall hide my reproach, and my name
shall be MAGDALEN POWER.
Never again shall I utter the name that I bore in
my childhood ;
Know it shall none, save the Angel that watched
at my christening hour.

8

Now I begin life again ; but a clearer, a stronger
    beginning :

Not as a child, but a woman—a teacher of children
    not mine.

What can *I* teach them ? *My* lesson ? Repenting
    is longer than sinning ?

Nay ; I can read ; I can write ; I can moralize,
    line upon line.

9

Branded no more as a felon :—but hush ! let such
    phrases be banished !

Let me recall the old precepts that moulded my
    innocent youth !

Knowledge, and Beauty, and Goodness, thank God !
    have not utterly vanished :

Quick to perceive them as ever ; alive to the glory
    of Truth.

10

No more abasement!   I'm weary and blind with the
   tears of repentance :
  Though it was wrong, and I know it, yet surely
   such weeping is vain.
Have I not borne to the full all the pangs of my
   terrible sentence ?
  Shall there no harvest arise from this plentiful
   penitent rain ?

11

Worshipping sorrow it seems, thus to sacrifice life on
   its altar ;
  Petting my error it is, thus to water it evening and
   morn :
Cherishing aye in my breast, as a fetish, a scarce
   escaped halter—
  This is the culture of Terror—Idolatry worthy of
   scorn !

12

I will no more of it.—Twenty-three years have I
 lived ; and my labour

Vanity, fruitless regret, and a secret that may not
 be told,

Honour-imperilling, head-overhanging, like Damocles'
 sabre,

Swinging and threat'ning my new-donned propriety
 scarce a day old.

13

Ha ! I must clothe me with armour ; yet not in the
 garb of defiance :

Panoply brazen flings back every incident ray of the
 sun :

Darkly encased I shall be in a corselet of quiet
 reliance ;

Shield I shall carry of triple propriety ; sword I'll
 have none.

14

Is this hypocrisy?   Is it a refuge 'twixt seeming and
    being?
  Self-enforced virtue (who knows?) may develop from
      habit to love.
Heedless of obstacles, patient for ends, strong of
    heart, and far-seeing,
  I may be wise as the serpent, yet innocent still as
      the dove.

15

Die then, sad memories, leaving behind you nor
    token nor relic!
  Hark how the tremulous night-wind is passing in
      joy-laden sighs!
Soft through my windows it comes, like the fanning
      of pinions angelic,
  Whispering to cease from myself, and look out on
      the infinite skies.

16

Out   on   the   orb-studded   night,   and   the   crescent
        effulgence of Dian;
   Out on the far-gleaming star-dust that marks where
        the angels have trod ;
Out on the gem-pointed Cross, and the glittering
        pomp of Orion,
   Flaming in measureless azure, the coronal jewels of
        God.

17

Luminous streams of delight in the silent immensity
        flowing,
   Journeying   surgelessly   on   through   impalpable
        ether of peace,
How can I think of myself when infinitude o'er me
        is glowing,
   Glowing with tokens of love from the land where
        my sorrows shall cease ?

18

Oh, summer-night of the South ! Oh, sweet languor

of zephyrs love-sighing !

Oh, mighty circuit of shadowy solitude, holy and

still !

Music scarce audible, echo-less harmony joyously

dying,

Dying in faint suspirations o'er meadow, and forest,

and hill !

19

I must go forth and be part of it, part of the night

and its gladness.

But a few steps, and I pause on the marge of the

shining lagoon.

Here then, at length, I have rest; and I lay down

my burden of sadness,

Kneeling alone 'neath the stars and the silvery

arc of the moon.

20

Peace-speaking night of the South, will thine in-
> fluence last through my sleeping,
>> Dream with my dreaming, awake with my waking,
>> and blend with the morn?

Or shall I start as of old, and my pillow be wet with
> my weeping,
>> Victim alternate of self-accusation and impious
>> scorn?

21

Have I so cast out myself that the morrow's meridian
> shall find me
>> Lightly esteeming the earth, and with spirit affianced
>> to heaven?

Have I said, once and for ever, " Proud Lucifer, get
> thee behind me !
>> Leave me to die in the desert, if only my sin be
>> forgiven "?

22

Let me not hoodwink myself. Of the many desires
that come thronging—

Demons they may be, or angels of brightness, I
hardly know which—

One I retain unto death, one supreme irresistible
longing ;

Heaven without it were poor, and earth with it
ineffably rich.

23

Can it be wrong? It was God, and not I, who
created me woman,

And on my woman's heart portrayed the nobler
ideal of man ;

Dowered me with instincts of love, that shall rule till
I cease to be human :

Shall the Creator require of the creature beyond
what she can?

24

Ah ! but the soft, subtle voice of the Night whispers,

"First be thou worthy :

Vaunt not thyself till the work of thy hands is

recorded above :

Gird thee for labour; and if, being earthly, thou

needs must be earthy,

Pray that through Duty alone thou attain to the

pleasaunce of love."

PLEASANTLY, almost too pleasantly, blendeth to-day with to-morrow.

Hours are as moments : a twinkle of white wings, and, lo, they are gone !

Day bringeth work without bondage, and night bringeth dreams without sorrow :

Pleasantly, almost too pleasantly, life is meandering on.

2

Precious my charge, and delightsome : three spirits
all joyous and tender—

Children of nature and innocence, breathing the
freshness of flowers.

Love-tokens are they from Paradise, warm from the
kiss of the Sender,

Blossoms of promise still rich with the glow of the
Amaranth Bowers.

3

Hyacinth, Lily, and Violet—pleasant conceit of their
christening :

Hyacinth, darkly embowered in the riches of
clustering curls ;

Slenderly delicate Lily, a lily transfigured and glistening ;

Violet, lowly and meek, yet the joy of my garland
of girls.

4

Happy their lot—in themselves, in their sire, in a
mother's affection ;
Happy in mutual love all the merry bright round
of the years,
Little they reck of the travailing world, with its
nameless dejection ;
Even their sighs are the surfeit of joy, laughter-
laden their tears.

5

Lofty things move them to worship ; adoring they
wonder, but fear not ;
Little things minister pleasure, as ever it fares with
the good ;
Nature to them utters low subtle voices that other
ears hear not ;
Marvellous harmonies greet them from river, and
mountain, and wood.

6

Down in umbrageous retreats, chosen haunts by the
    shadow-flecked river,
Drinking delights from the murmur of streams and
    ⸱ the flutter of wings,
Streams as they murmur, bright wings as they flutter,
    green leaves as.they quiver,
All have strange music for them, and a tale of
    invisible things.

7

Almost I fancy them other than human; great
    Nature's own daughters,
Beings of Fable that only the rapture of Fancy
    conceives,
Naiad-like, laving white feet in the dimpled disturbance
    of waters,
Dryad-like, peering bright-visioned thro' tremulous
    umbrage of leaves.

8

Otherwhile mounted on steeds and in madness of
motion careering,

Fitfully seen thro' far vistas, and mazy divergence
of trees;

Elfin-revealings of fleetness and liberty sudden
appearing,

Vanishing whither they list, uncontrolled as the
libertine breeze.

9

Train them and form them! Ah me! it is they who,
unconscious, have wrought me

Back to the form that I bore when I bloomed as
the darling of home.

I their preceptress! Ah me! with their innocent
smiles they have taught me

Lessons more glorious than Greece, aspirations
more lofty than Rome.

10

Mine is the love of dark ages, of empires convulsed
and war-wasted,

Rapine and bloodshed, the ebb and the flow of
perpetual strife;

I of the Tree of the Knowledge of Good and of
Evil have tasted;

Fitter for *them* were the fruit of the Tree, angel-
guarded, of Life.

HYACINTH loves . . . I have noted of late the
mysterious transition ;
Soft silken-footed approaches of something that
whispers a change ;
Chrysalis-stirrings that herald the full-winged and
perfected mission ;
Timid assumptions of woman-demeanour unwonted
and strange ;

2

Beautiful sequence of vermeil suffusions and paleness
    unbidden ;
  Dream-lustred eyes that look inward on something
    to others unseen ;
Reveries sudden, and maidenly languor, and sighs
    but half-hidden ;
  Pensive reserve over-drooping the virginal grace of
    her mien.

3

Saddened, yet listlessly happy ; ah, well I remember
    the token !
  Well I remember the oxymel mingling of pleasure
    and pain !
Some face hath gleamed upon hers, and the sleep of
    her childhood is broken ;
  Hardly she knows as yet whether to rise or to
    slumber again.

IV.

WANDERING to-day by the river where refuge
　　is greenest and coolest,
　Watching beneath me the moving mosaic of
　　shadow and sheen,
Came I on Hyacinth, radiant, elated, her bloom at
　　the fullest,
　Rapt, like a vision-filled soul that hath quaffed of
　　divine Hippocrene.

2

No need of words to interpret those moist lips
 half-parted and glowing,
 Nor the luxurious droop of the eye-lid with
  pleasure opprest,
Nor the strewn wealth of her tresses, in careless
 dishevelment flowing,
 Nor the warm crimson that blushed thro' the
  gossamer folds on her breast.

3

Heedless and hearing not, trance-like—the sun thro'
 the bowerage above her,
 Scattering broken effulgence, like largesse of gold,
  on her charms,—
Stood the flushed impress of maidenhood fresh from
 the kiss of a lover,
 Fervid in recent release from the passioned
  entwinement of arms.

4

Such I divined, with an eye and an instinct for Love's

hidden history;

Thrilled by ineffable sympathies, every sweet token

I knew,

Gathered in fancy the fluttering threads, and unravelled

the mystery,

Read, like a scroll, the yet lingering signs of

reluctant adieu.

5

Lower her eyelids drooped, closing; then rose, and

the sensuous present

Broke once again into verdure and song, on her

eye and her ear;

But the entrancement of vision was gone, and the

bloom evanescent

Passed into sorrowful paleness, and died in the

track of a tear.

6

Then, while her ringlets, in silken compliance and
    rich adaptation,
  Rounded each movement with graces, as music the
    words of a lay,
Stooped she a moment, and, fluttering still with Love's
    sweet trepidation,
  Caught up a scroll from the grass at her feet, and
    moved, sighing, away.

7

And, till the sun set, empurpling the glorified hills
    with its splendour,
  Lone in her chamber sat Hyacinth, writing the
    words on her soul ;
Then, as the glory died, yielding to radiance more
    softened and tender,
  Forth from her chamber came Hyacinth, singing
    the song of the scroll :

8

"Ever thou speakest of angels, my love, and I fear
me, I fear me,

Thou art too heavenly pure to commèrce with
such grossness as mine."

"Angels are lower than God, and when thou art
anear me, anear me,

Godhead looks into mine eyes, for thy kinship,
through grace, is Divine."

9

"Ah, but the angels will find thee in sleep, and will
take thee, will take thee,

Bearing thee far from me, leaving me weary,
forsaken, and old."

"Yea, but thou likewise shalt sleep, and my singing
shall wake thee, shall wake thee,

Over the crystalline sea, by the city of jasper and
gold."

10

" Ah, but the angels are better than I ! and will love
thee, will love thee,

Teaching thee music I know not, and whispering
secrets of bliss."

" Yea, but though angels, no angel I'll cherish above
thee, above thee ;

Nought, till thou come to thy love, save the feet of
my God, shall I kiss."

11

" Ah, but the angels, the iris-winged angels, will hate
me, will hate me,

Soiled with the touch of corruption, and swathed
in the cerements of sin."

" Nay, at the glistening portals of pearl I'll await thee,
await thee,

Bearing thee radiant attire for the joy of thine
entering in."

12

"Ah, but the angels, the aurioled angels, adoring,
adoring,

Will they not mock us, faint-quiring the notes of
our penitent strain?"

" Nay, for our hymns have a theme of Redemption,
high-soaring, high-soaring,

Far o'er the music of angels, the song of the Lamb
that was slain."

*   *   *   *   *   *

13

"Where hath she learned it?" quoth one ; and "Who
wrote it? who gave it ?" another :

Hyacinth answered with silvery laughter, and sought
her lone room.

" Surely my child has some secret at heart," said the
wondering mother.

I alone knew why she brooked not the question of
whence or by whom.

14

All the night-long in her slumber I heard the
unconscious out-pouring

Of her young spirit in jubilant thoughts from the
dream-broken strain ;

Ever she murmured—" a theme of Redemption high-
soaring, high-soaring,

Far o'er the music of angels, the song of the Lamb
that was slain."

V.

"PLEASANTLY," said I? Yea, pleasantly.
Three summer months of contentment,
Bright with bright faces, and sweet with sweet
voices, or sleeping in smiles.
Here the green earth is the heaven-domed temple of
poet's presentment,
Manifold harmonies rolling for ever thro' long
forest aisles.

2

Softly I've moved through the time with the echo-less
footfalls of Duty,
Wearing the garments of meekness and schooling
; my heart to constraint,
Shunning my mirror for dread of the slumbering
demon of Beauty :
Puritan I in my plainness of garb, in demeanour
a saint.

3

All I resolved I have done much in spirit, and
wholly in letter ;
Faultless my conduct and converse . . . but where
is the sign of return ?
See, I have prisoned my life in routine till my soul is
no better
Than the grey ashes that lie in the coldly-
symmetrical urn.

4

Am I then weary of well-doing, deeming it fruitless
endurance?
Nay, but my spirit is cloyed with the feast of
perpetual sweets.
I was not moulded for peace, or the dreamless repose
of assurance.
Oh, I am faint with the opiate breath of these
woodland retreats!

5

This is not life, to be bowed in the heart-hush of
worship for ever,
Softly asleep on my shadow to glide o'er a
summer-lit sea.
Life is not passionless calm, but the turbid delight of
the river.
Give me the billowy Jordan! . . . enough now of
blue Galilee.

6

All my young dream was of heroes; my play was
  Olympian frolic,

  Venus, Minerva, Alecto, alternate—love, wisdom,
    and gall.

What is the mood of my life-music now? Why, a
  piping bucolic,

  Babbling melodious of pastoral peace and content;
    that is all.

7

Soul cannot march to the bleating of sheep and the
  lowing of cattle.

  Rather the war-blast were thrilling again in mine
    ears!

Oh for a touch of the palpitant world! for the glory
  of battle!

  Show me once more the proud wave of the
    banners, the gleam of the spears!

8

What would I conquer ?   Myself ?   So I might ; but
such war were inglorious.

How should it yield me the rapture that only the
conqueror feels ?

What were the spoils of the slain ?   To what Capitol
march when victorious ?

Whom should I drag thro' the dust, captive-bound
at my chariot-wheels ?

9

Oh, I am sick of unlaurelled self-conquest !   A region
fire-smitten

Lies at the feet of the victor, unworthy the cost of
the strife.

What is the fruit of my summer of meekness ?
Behold, I have *written !*

Ink ! where the blood should have been, and the
dust of the battle of life !

10

Stay. Let me question myself. Whence this change
 of mood? Yesterday only
All in my heart was the hush of the temple,
 ＇ conventual calm.
Yesterday quickening Nature sufficed me; alone, but
 not lonely,
Breathing concordant with all things, embraced in
 the infinite psalm.

11

Now all this musical silence but frets me. I live, but
 I sing not,
Save in harsh discords that jar with the tender
 discourse of the flowers.
Soft airs are wooing my brow with their winnowing
 wings, but they bring not
Tribute of hope. Time's too smooth, and I chafe
 at the impotent hours.

12

What hath unfellowed me thus from the spirits of
beauty beside me?
Why do I turn from the honey of life to the
blood-kindling wine?
Yesterday, heaven was opened: I saw, but its bliss
was denied me,
Saw it in Hyacinth's eyes with the Demon of Envy
in mine.

13

Even as she passed from my sight, while the branches
yet shook from her presence,
Rose in unblest resurrection the sepulchred passions
of yore.
I to go dreaming of life while this novice is drinking
its essence!
I to be almost content with the dregs, while her
cup runneth o'er!

14

Say, were an angel cast down by mischance at the
  great consummation,
Would not his sharpest distress be the gleam of his
      home in the skies ?
Even the shadow of heaven were worse torment than
  hell's conflagration :
What then for me was the reflex of Eden in
  Hyacinth's eyes !

15

Shut out from life and from love by hard circumstance,
  not from unmeetness,
Can I untempted look on while another sits down
  to the feast ?
Why must I drag through the hours when this
  Hyacinth leaps to completeness,
Leaps to her queenly meridian, still flushed with
  the roseate east ?

16

"It is because thou hast sinned." Oh emaciate
ghost of repentance !
Thou here again with thine offerings of sackcloth,
and ashes, and tears!
Pointing thy skeleton finger at Law ! See, I
point to the Sentence,
Paid to the uttermost farthing by weary fulfilment
of years.

17

What then? Shall envy inherit me wholly? A
thousand times Never.
It hath but waked me once more from the spell
of a somnolent hour,
Stirred up the thorns in the nest, struck a spur in
the flank of endeavour :
I am the old self again. I am. . . . Nay, I am
Magdalen Power.

!

VI.

STRANGERS to-day ; a momentous event in
   this slumb'rous seclusion :
Lily and Violet sadly impatient of precept and
   books :
Hyacinth calmer, but fluttering dove-like with pretty
   confusion ;
Something of mystery, too, in those quick interro-
   gative looks.

2

" Are they from far?" I ask carelessly.   " Not from a

very great distance,"

Violet answers ; " but oh ! 'tis so seldom they visit

us now.

There was a quarrel, you know," she continues with

prattling persistence,

All unaware of the shadow that gathers on

Hyacinth's brow.

3

" Something I don't understand, about cattle. and

buying, and selling ;

Arthur Trevelyan was rude, and dropped words

about 'ill-gotten gear' ;

Father was angered, and said that no Convict should

darken his dwelling :

But he repented, and wrote to both father and son :

so they're here.

4

"What is a Convict?" she asks me; "Trevelyan's a
    Convict, they tell me.
It must be something, I'm sure, to be proud of, if
    Raymond is one."
Ah, cruel question that would to my own definition
    compel me!
Hyacinth comes to my rescue: "A Convict!
    Young Raymond is none!

5

"Tell me," she said, and I mark the unwonted and
    quivering passion,
    "Can it be just that a son should inherit a father's
      disgrace?"
Gladly I catch at the turn of the theme, and reply,
      "'Tis a fashion
That were best honoured by breach." There's
    a story in Hyacinth's face.

VII.

OFT hath it pleased me in day-dream and night-
watch to mould an ideal :

Is not my heart-wish incarnate, new-risen or dropt
from above ?

One sudden gleam of a face, and my cherished ideal
is real !

There moved my miracle, there passed my Fate,
whom to see is to love !

2

Somewhere I've read that the gods, waxing wroth at
  our mad importunity,
  Hurl us our boon, and it falls with the weight of a
    curse at our feet :
Perilous thing to intrude on their lofty Olympian
  immunity !
  "Take it, and die," say the gods, and we die of
    our fondest conceit.

3

Is it so now with myself? I have riven the night-
  watches asunder,
  Murmuring "Give me to see him," and fretting
    the beautiful skies.
Lo, I have seen him ! And now, I shrink,
  trembling with impotent wonder,
  Pondering, Is it the blessing I craved, or a curse in
    disguise ?

4

Yes, I have seen him ; and envious murmur and
fretful rebellion

Pause as I muse on a possible future, and gird up
my strength.

How my wild spirit was hushed when I looked on
this Raymond Trevelyan !

Prince of my dreams, by the throb of this heart,
thou art come—come at length !

VIII.

DOWN in the vines he is sitting, the fruitage
leaf-shadowed above him

Lending concomitant charm to the ripeness that
flushes his cheek.

There is the glory of summer about him. I see
him, and love him,

Asking not why. I but know that the strong one
is come to the weak.

D

2

Down in the vines he is sitting; and radiance leaf-
softened and golden

On the broad calm of his brow through the veil of
the vintage is shed.

Blest be each bough that enshrines him!   Henceforth
I am ever beholden

Unto the slenderest, tenderest leaflet that shelters
his head.

3

Down in the vines he is sitting; I see him leaf-circled
and Faun-like,

Such as I've seen in my dreams, in like halo of
amber and green,

With those same love-seeking glances, so placidly,
dreamily, dawn-like,   .

Quiet as the birth of the dew, as the star of the
morning serene.

4

Dream, heart, no more of thy lyre-lauded heroes, and
    demi-gods storied !
Open thine eyes on the breathing fulfilment of
    beauty and strength !
Down in the vines he is sitting; I see him leaf-girt,
    and leaf-gloried ;
Prince of my dreams, by the throb of this heart,
    thou art come—come at length !

IX

ONLY two syllables uttered—"Goodnight;" a
conventional pressure—

Nay, not so much—a mere meeting of finger-tips
formally deigned.

Nothing for heart to interpret; no look to remember
and treasure :

Lovingly courteous to others; to me alone coldly
constrained.

2

Yet he is mine.   I have marked him for mine.
     Am I fantasy's minion?
  Slave to a self-born philosophy? victim of doating
       conceit?
Or, am I privileged priestess, beholding dark things
     Eleusinian,
  Piercing the thought of the gods, and fore-casting
     the way of their feet?

3

Gods, gods, and gods!   I am weary of gods!   I have
     looked on humanity,
  Living, and breathing, and glowing, and burning.
     limb, body, and face!
Time that my dreams become touch, that I cease
     from this bodiless vanity,
  Wistfully rounding my vacuous arms to the shape
     of embrace!

X.

OVER my mirror. 'Tis time that I look to my
weapons and armour.

Keener than ever, I fancy, the penetrant edge of
my glance.

I can remember a fuller-orbed cheek, and a rose-
blushing warmer ;

But on my brow is no line sorrow-furrowed, no
wake of mischance.

2

Loves he dark tresses, I wonder, in sinuous subtlety
    twining?
Loves he dark eyes, fired with love, and star-
    sympathied passion of night?
Loves he the long drooping eye-lash, half secret half
    story combining?
Loves he the lithe grace of undulous ease, and
    imperial height?

3

This is the reflex of beauty I gaze on, the beauty
    I've hidden,
Most from myself, and have struggled thro' years of
    control to forget,
Deeming it e'en as a perilous thing, and a weapon
    forbidden,
Piercing the hand of the user, and dealing but
    shame and regret.

4

Wherefore should beauty be evil? and that which in
 lilies and roses
 Men deem most gracious and holy be fatal in
  woman alone?
Why should the flower seek the light, while the
 woman in cloister reposes,
 Sealed down by vows from the eyes that were made
  to drink love at her own?

5

Beauty, like Knowledge, is Power; what of Beauty
 and Knowledge colleaguing,
 Guided by keen-visioned Prudence to work to one
  ultimate goal?
Not Cleopatra herself, 'mid the lurements of Tarsus
 intriguing,
 Boasted this tri-une endowment concluded in body
  and soul.

6

Not as my past is my present.   No more as a child
　　shall I stumble,
　Hastening the end by false measures, and grasping
　　　the fruit immature :
I shall be patient.   The time may be long, and the
　　means may be humble,
　But he is mine ; I have marked him for mine ; and
　　the triumph is sure.

7

This idle curl that I smooth even now betwixt finger
　　and finger
　Silkenly circling his own shall he press upon
　　amorous lips ;
Yea, on the yielding delight of this breast shall that
　　conquered head linger,
　And 'neath the veil of these tresses lie hid in
　　enamoured eclipse.

8

But my lamp pales as I gaze; and I feel the weird

    tremor that thrilleth

  Brain, heart, and limb, when the night seems to

    yield up its soul unto day.

Now to mine orisons.   Shall I then speak as the

    spirit not willeth ?

  Nay: I must couch me unshriven.   To-night I am

    powerless to pray.

!

XI.

WAS it a chance or a Providence brought me
   once more to the river?
Wandering whither I knew not, and cared not, I
   came as before
Unto the spot. It was ever my solace to wander;
   and ever
Seem I allured to the stream : for the rush and the
   musical roar,

2

Rhyming and chiming in mystic agreement with that
which works in me,

Bravely concording with thoughts of wild action
and furious delight,

Win me from baleful contentment, from dreamy
oblivion win me,

Call me to live and to dare, re-endow me with
motion and might.

3

How I have smiled at my school-bred compatriots
languidly viewing

Ivy-clad relics caducous, and morbidly learned in
decay !

Give me the bountiful rush of my river, its ever-
renewing

Life and festivity, song, dance, and revel by night
and by day !

4

Surely 'twas this and not espionage guided my fanciful

wandering,

Drew me thro' bosky entanglement e'en to the

ripple-wooed marge;

Couched me in ready concealment, and set me

conjecturing, pondering,

Ever on life, and on *my* life; when, lo, by the

mangroves a barge

5

Fairy-like, noiselessly gliding!   Or ever I saw

him I knew him.

Knew by the sudden rebound of my blood, and the

quiver of limb!

Knew, too, that rustling of leaves, and the gleam of

white vesture that drew him

Unto the haven appointed—the heaven of Hyacinth

and him.

6

Then the old story, the Adam-old story, the Eve-old
love story :
Rapture of lips, and entwining of arms, and
commingling of sighs,
Heart-to-heart clingings, and glad jets of tears ; all the
glow and the glory
Of a ripe summer of love sunned in splendour of
amorous eyes.

7

Was it in generous forbearance I bore me so calmly,
so mildly,
Marking the kiss-dented lips, and sweet license of
zephyr-blown hair ?
Who could have dreamed of young Hyacinth clasping
and clinging so wildly ?
She of the angels ! In sooth such embracement is
not of the air.

8

Well : 'tis enough. A new obstacle. Sometimes the
    ghost of it haunted me,
  Breathing on sparks of suspicion that now are
    enkindled to flame.
Phantom no more : I have seen, and the glare of the
    truth hath not daunted me ;
  Truly, forewarned is forearmed, and I grow but the
    more to mine aim.

9

She is a child ; I a woman ; and he ! could he fill up
    the measure
  Of the great longing I read in his eyes with a kiss
    or a song?
Greatness of heart soon outgrows the milk-dainties of
    infantile pleasure.
  Weak silly-winning young ways are poor wiles for
    the wise and the strong.

10

It is not ivy he needeth, the boughs of his manhood
caressing,

Ivy that drains what it clings to, and sappeth the
life of the tree.

It is the earth for the roots, and the blood of the
storm, and the blessing

Wrapt in the rolling of vapours, and born of the
sun and the sea.

11

These would I give him, a closer embrace than poor
parasite clinging,

Being his meat, and his drink, and his strength, and
his light, and his breath !

Is not this better than daintiest love-lore of sighing
and singing ?

Hyacinth ! Hyacinth !   It is not you, it is I
. . . his till death !

12

Yea, though I saw you to-day in the rapture of
parasite-clinging,

Luring the strength from his heart, and suspiring a
mutual breath,

Practising daintiest love-lore of kissing, and sighing,
and singing,

Hyacinth! Hyacinth! . . . it is not you . . . it is
I . . . his till death!

XII.

LET me be justified in my own sight. She is
young, and before her
Lies all the wide world to choose from. Would
God that it were so with me !
Hers is blind impulse : she cannot have chosen : and
Raymond reigns o'er her
Only by right of first comer. Not such would my
fealty be !

2

Not with the eye of a child do I measure those
opulent merits—
Frame of Antinöus, utterance of Pericles, heart of
!   " The Just."
All the more mine do I claim him because of the
taint he inherits :
This were a shame unto her in high places of
blue-veined disgust.

3

Shall I invoke higher motives, and sanction my
purpose by duty?
Well, an I would, so I might, and no more than
my duty fulfil.
Am not I Hyacinth's keeper, aedile of this temple of
beauty,
Bound by my service and honour to watch and to
guard? . . . And I *will.*

XIII.

LINGER, oh Sun, for a little, nor close yet this
    day of a million !
  Is there not glory enough in the rose-curtained halls
    of the West ?
Hast thou no joy in the passion-hued folds of thy
    kingly pavilion ?
  Why shouldst thou only pass through it ? Oh
    rest thee a little while, rest !

2

Why should the Night come and take it, the wan
Night that cannot enjoy it,

Bringing pale argent for golden, and changing
vermilion to grey?

Why should the Night come and shadow it, entering
but to destroy it?

Rest 'mid thy ruby-trailed splendours! Oh stay
thee a little while, stay!

3

Rest thee at least a brief hour in it! 'Tis a right
royal pavilion.

Lo, there are thrones for high dalliance all
gloriously canopied o'er!

Lo, there are hangings of purple, and hangings of
blue and vermilion,

And there are fleeces of gold for thy feet on the
diapered floor!

4　　　　　　　.

Linger, a little while linger. To-morrow my heart
    may not sing to thee :
This shall be Yesterday, numbered with memories,
    folded away.
Now should my flesh-fettered soul be set free ! I
    would soar to thee, cling to thee,
And be thy rereward Aurora, pursuing the skirts of
    To-day !

5

Shall I not doat on to-day that hath brought me the
    earnest of blessing,
Young buds of friendship whose promise the
    coming of time shall fulfil ?
First the green blade ; then the ear, from the green to
    the yellow progressing ;
Then the full corn in the ear, golden-waving, to
    reap when I will.

6

For, as it fell out to-day, I was sought and was found
  of young Raymond ;
And he hath told me his story, beseeching my
  counsel and aid :
Closest of friends, we are Pythias out-Pythias'd and
  Damon out-Damon'd ;
Man unto man is as nought to our friendship of
  young man and maid.

7

All this is well. It is something to nourish a secret
  between us.
All this is well. There are meetings, and moon-
  light and star-light in store.
Ah, my poor "mournful Œnone," dost think there is
  pity in Venus
When she contends with her peers for the prize?
  Such have I, and no more.

8

This is not new in the love-lore of woman—love's
    messenger pleading
  Subtly and warily, making the cause of another her
    own ;
Skilfully pouring in shaft upon shaft, till the love that
    lies bleeding
  Turns to the smiter for help, and finds rest in her
    bosom alone.

9

Didst thou not dream then, my love, when I proffered
    a guerdonless traffic
  'Twixt that poor dove and thyself, that thy trust was
    most sweetly beguiled ?
Didst thou then deem me so icy-angelic, so snowy-
    seraphic,
  That I but gazed on thine eyes to reflect back
    their light on a child ?

10

Ah me! this turmoil of heart! Is it truly a change
  for the better?

Once I remember a setting of sun, yea, and
  settings of suns,

Which I all-hailed, when-as warder, and order, and
  grating, and fetter,

Passed into darkness and silence—twin-heaven of
  the spirit that shuns.

11

Daylight and audible life. Oh my soul! the delight,
  the delicious

Pressing together of arms, and up-gathering of
  knees to the chin,

And the spent air breathed for warmth 'twixt the
  breasts, while the darkness propitious

Softer than wool wrapt me round with a dreamless
  oblivion of sin!

12

Which is the better?—the torpid collapse of spent
penitence crouching

Into the darkness and solitude, hugging the joy of
the night,

Or the fierce gladness of day that would hinder the
sun from his couching,

Mad with the bitter-sweet wine of desire, and the
pain of delight?

13

Is there no midway for such one as I am 'twixt being
and doing?

Is there no choice save the lotus of sleep or the
apple of strife?

Is there no bliss that is neither dull rest nor a fevered
pursuing?

Is there no twilight dividing the noon-flame and
night of my life?

14

Well, what I am, that I am.   It is better to scheme

than to slumber.

What was this goodness that sometime I strove

⸮   for?   Supineness, constraint,

Mortification of spirit, and crosses and thorns without

number,

Pride in abasement, and sombre complacence of

embryo saint.

15

That is all over; and, saving some fitful remembrance

of pity

Piercing the joints of the harness, to break as it

reaches the heart,

All is as erst. . . .   Touching Hyacinth, she must to

school, to the city.

This I advise for her good—for her good (perhaps

mine, too, in part).

XIV

VASTNESS of verdurous solitude, forest com-
    plexity boundless,

Where is no stir save the fall of a leaf, or the wave

of a wing :

Lone sunny regions where virginal Nature roams

ceaseless and soundless,

Rich with the richness of summer, yet fresh with

the freshness of spring :

2

Where is no stir save of leaf in its falling, or bird in
  its winging,
  Or the unfrequent sweet idyll low-murmured by
  ♪   devious streams ;
Where is no passion, or sign of desire, save the
  infantile clinging
  Of the young tendrils, or opening of flowers to a
  morning of beams.

3

That was but yesterday.   Comes a brief journey . . .
  a sleep . . . and the morrow
  Wakes on the City, with issuing forth of tumultuous
  life—
Wakes upon quickening footsteps, and faces acquainted
  with sorrow,
  Hurried uptaking of burdens, and voices familiar
  with strife.

4

Marvel of contrast, that seems like the swift incoher-
ence of vision!

As peradventure it may be ; for who can say more
than " It seems "?

Surely all life is a dream, mis-begot of Olympian
derision,

And the divided strange courses of men are but
dreams within dreams.

5

Let me dream on, then.   Of late I confess I have
dreamed somewhat pleasantly.

Last night I dreamed of a school in a convent.
And Hyacinth and I

Came to the gate.   So we knocked at the gate, and
it opened, and presently

Hyacinth passed from my sight, and I heard a voice
sobbing " Good-bye."

6

Poor little Hyacinth! But it was better, assuredly

better.

You'll be too busy to think, and too much with

!   the angels to care.

Now you are safe from the freaks of young fantasy—

safe as your letter

Is *not* to pass from my hand into his. You'll forget

him in there!

XV

BACK to my woods; back to Lily and Violet;
back to the daily

Track of the wheels, and the hidden rotation of

wheels within wheels.

But there is hush in the home all unwonted. Where

three voices gaily

Sang to one tune, there is silence, save whispers,

and wordless appeals

2

From sad young eyes unto mine, as the last who have
    seen and have kissed her,
  Fretting my soul with unspoken entreaty and
    inquest of truth,
Seeming to ask with sharp scrutiny "What hast thou
    done with our sister?
  Art thou more cruel than death, that thou grudgest
    the years of her youth?"

3

Give me a woman to strive with, a man, or a demon,
    or angel!
  When did I tremble or cringe, when the proud and
    the strong were my foes?
But from the weaklings of Christ, from the delicate
    lambs of Evangel,
  From the lorn looks of young innocents—save me,
    oh save me from those!

PART SECOND.

I.

EVEN as water to him who thirsts wayfaring,
dust-dry and burning,
After sore heat and long stumbling in courses with
never a rill,
Weary with counting of ridges, and barren result of
much turning,
Tempted to curse God and die, let the afterward
be what it will;

2

Even as the brimming delight of the wine-cup by fair
hands commended

Unto hot lips that are sanguine from onslaught and,
stiff-set from ire,

With the undoing of baldrick and habergeon heavy
and splendid,

Changed for a girth of white arms, and the softness
of silken attire;

3

Even as pressure of ministering hands on the fevered
and aching

Brow of the sorrowful, morrow-full sire and provider
of bread,

Wherein is grace of sweet solace and peace, and a
virtue awaking

Unexplained hope, and discernment of bliss all
around and o'er-head;

4

Even as green rivage with homestead, rose-garden,
     and grass-lawn trim-shaven,
Unto eyes weary with wide waste of waters and
     seething sea-foam,
Changing the spirit of heaviness into the joy of the
     haven,
And the long vigils of storm to the rest and
     observance of home ;

5

Even as the stirring of leaves on the boughs after
     breathless unbroken
Months of dead drought, when the earth is as iron,
     and heaven as brass,
When the rain-argosy cometh, and sendeth a sigh for
     a token,
And there is hope in the flowers, and a wave on
     the languishing grass ;

6

Even as the coming of dawn to the pilgrims in
 trackless wild places,
 Lighting up landmarks of old, and confirming his
 face to the south
Zionward,—even to Jerusalem the Golden, where rest
 is and grace is,
 Whither he toils, angel-tended, with Songs of
 Degrees in his mouth ;

7

Even as the coming of night to the premature
 children of labour,
 Smit to the heart of their youth with the curse
 of the iron and steel—
Night with re-unions of home, or sweet converse of
 neighbour with neighbour,
 Proffering the peace of her stars for the wildering
 whirl of the wheel ;

8

Even as all golden moments, all joyance of welcome

transition,

Gathered from all the wide circuit of life and

concluded in one;—

So to Love's fever and fret, its sore travail and

thirsting ambition,

Comes what my lips and my heart knew to-day at

the set of the sun !

HE is not faithless or fickle, and had he all
    shamelessly yielded
  At the first stroke, I had spurned him, and left
    him ignobly to die :
Or I had dallied a little, and played with the potence
    I wielded—
  Kissed him perchance, and then loathed him, and
    branded his love with a lie.

2

I might have gazed on his eyes till the light of
　　allurement had quenched them;
　Suffered a violent brief little bondage of manly
　　 ¡ embrace;
This way and that way have parted his hair with my
　　fingers, then clenched them,
　And with the scorn of a woman have smitten him
　　full on the face.

3

But he is noble and virtuous, patient of evil appear-
　　ance;
　Charity in him is sovereign; it suffereth long and
　　is kind.
"She may seem wholly estranged; all is darkness;
　　but time bringeth clearance,
　And I will grope in my darkness, content for her
　　sake to be blind."

4

Long months of silence, and agonized waiting, and
ever-increasing

Substance of wonder still found him believing the
message would come :

Yet not as mine could his suffering be, a hid torture
unceasing,

Knowing the cause, yea, and *being* the cause, and
yet wilfully dumb.

5

Ah those poor letters of his and of hers !   Like things
murdered they haunt me.

Dead things have power on me, though with the
quick I be fearless and brave.

Surely the fire would consume them !   But how if
the sight of them daunt me !

And when I open my desk, it would seem as I
opened a grave.

6

There are some things even I cannot do. False I
could not declare her ;
Nor could I ruthlessly slander a living love never
withdrawn.
How could I rail at poor Hyacinth, knowing her
purer and fairer
In the well-springs of her soul than the opaline
deeps of the dawn ?

7

Thanks to her father, her blundering father, who
spoke of her marriage,
Right in the hearing of Raymond, as something
quite fixed and at hand :
Vulgarly boasted of fortune in store for her, "servants
and carriage,"
And of the change of her name to a name that is
known in the land.

8

Thanks to her father, who knows not the obstacle,
  knows not the wayward
    Heart of a girl that no arbiter brooks in the gift
    of her youth ;
Sees not, gold-dazzled, the scorn of the world when
    December looks Mayward ;
    Thanks to her father mistaking his easy consent
    for the truth.

9

Hyacinth seen, and admired, and desired—this I
    knew, and concealed it ;
    Fain would have shaped it to something, and
    profited somehow thereby ;
Made it available, made her seem saleable, subtly
    revealed it :
    Thanks to the old man again, who has saved me
    the crime of a lie.

10

This was the spark.   It was not of my lighting.

    Mine only to breathe on it.

Ready the fuel, long-dried by suspense, to flame

    into a hell!

Mine but to watch the dark cauldron of agony bubble

    and seethe on it,

Then to sing soft incantations that loosen and

    alter the spell.

11

Wherefore record them: the wiles and the low-

    whispered counsel, the honeyed

Words of feigned comfort, the maxims of wisdom,

    the fanning of pride,

Praises disguised as dispraise of alliances landed and

    moneyed—

Damning excuses, replete with exposure, while

    seeming to hide?

12

Wherefore ?   There are, and myself am of such, who
     are slaves to an inward

   Devil of self-contemplation that drinks its own
        blood and own breath,

Lapping insatiate at all streams alike, be they God-
        ward or sinward;

   Making good evil, bad worse : self-consuming, yet
        frugal of death.

13

Even as the shedder of blood ever fleeing the dread
        scene of slaughter,

   Yet by centripetal charm ever drawn to the spot
        where the hand

Points from the shuddering earth, or the sodden
        white face on the water

   Stares its unsinking appeal till his days be cut off
        from the land,—

14

So do I circle and hover, so flee, and yet circle and
　　hover
　Round my past deeds, and past purpose, and
　　central arcana of sin.
When shall I know the great sigh of relief, the
　　" Thank God, it is over "?
　Ah, could I think death were better how soon
　　should I slumber therein !

15

Strange I should love to record what, already too
　　luridly lettered,
　Burns on the tablets within me in lines of un-
　　quenchable fire.
Strange there is respite in singing of self, that the
　　Demon sleeps fettered,
　When of my passion-strained heart-strings I make
　　me and wake me a lyre.

G

16

Even as I've seen in fair Italy, where the weird
mystical mountain
Travailing mightily foams with red ruin from
summit to base;
Seen there the cunning in art, ere destruction is
quenched at its fountain,
Take of the lava, and make of it things of adorn-
ment and grace;

17

Yea, of the spume of convulsion make things to be
worn on the bosom,
Out of the travail of darkness bring issue of beauty
to light,
Fashion a dove into tenderness, simulate softness
of blossom,
Or the fair shoulders of Sappho, voluptuous,
Parian-white;

18

So do I take of my sin, and my suffering, and labour
    of passion,
    Mould them to semblance of beauty of Nature, or
    classic conceit,
Smooth them, and lose me the body of pain in the
    sense of the fashion,
    Binding distress itself captive to art in the linking
    of feet.

19

Yet, to re-track all the wiles one by one—nay I
    cannot, I may not.
    Under the web is complexity, subtle, and hopeless
    to trace.
Raymond is blameless.   How could he be else!
    There are things that I say not
    Which would redeem him in eyes the severest
    from ban of disgrace.

III.

DID not I dream that true happiness sat in the throne of attainment,
Crowned with the crown of victorious endeavour, and sceptred with palm?
Did not I see Fate herself flower-subdued, and in rosy enchainment,
And the importunate problem of life lying stifled in balm?

2

Is it the way of high Heaven to mock us with tokens
of favour,

Lavish of sunshine to ripen the growth of our
dearest device ;

Then to deceive us with harvests that nourish not,
fruits without savour,

Hemlock and hebenon clothed with the semblance
of balsam and spice ?

3

Is the high God of Evangel more cruel than gods
of old fable ?

Tantalus only *beholds*, never touches, the fruit ere
it slips :

But this Jehovah—He filleth our hands with it,
heapeth our table ;

Then laughs in heaven when it changes to ashes
and fire on our lips !

4

Yes ; turn on Heaven !   Call the gods, then the God
of gods, scornful and cruel !
Rail at the pitiless Triads that rule us, and mock
us, and curse !
Call up thine ancient despair, challenge Nemesis'
self to the duel !
Arm thee with Greek old-world blasphemies ! . . .
Feel'st thou then better, or worse ?

5

Thou hast the wish of thine heart.   Would'st have
more ?   See, 'twixt finger and finger,
Lo, how he twineth thy hair, and then lifts it to
amorous lips !
See, on the yielding delight of thy breast doth the
conquered head linger,
And 'neath the veil of thy tresses lies hid in
enamoured eclipse !

6

Wherefore the fret?   Is it surfeit of pleasure or surfeit
>   of sinning?
Would'st thou have appetite grow with the feeding?
>   the lust of the eyes
Ever renewed with the gazing?   And knew'st thou
>   not from the beginning
That, when sin hath its desire, the desirableness
>   thereof dies?

7

Is it God's way that in Nature He suffereth His own
>   disappearance,
Leaves it to work to its end in the groove of
>   immutable rule ;
But that in things of the spirit He willeth direct
>   interference,
Giving the crown to the simple, and meting out
>   grace to the fool?

8

Is this His sovereign and awful prerogative : joy He
retaineth

Absolute, in His own hands, to bestow, to withhold,
to destroy ?

What shall it profit a man that he prosper, if joy *He*
restraineth

Who can give joy without cause, and a bounteous
cause without joy ?

9

I am a fool to indulge me in sadness of spirit-
communing.

Thought is all sadness ; but night is all kindness :
the stars are on high.

It is the hour.   I will rush to him, cling to him, revel
to swooning

In the dear love of him.   Eat, drink, be merry,
To-morrow we die !

IV.

WHAT have I gained? One grand moment, one
moment supreme and delirious.

Something hath perished from earth and from
heaven since that eve when he spoke :

That one prime eve, when the moon was a sun, and
the brightness of Sirius

Glowed in the tiniest star, and the palpitant
firmament broke

2

Everywhere into confusion of glory, and sordid
conditions,

Earthy and palpable, clean fell away from our feet
and our eyes,

And in the mid air we seemed, ether-fed with unspeakable visions,

And there was none save us twain in the lands, or
the seas, or the skies !

3

Now is no life at my heart save the life of the serpent
that hisses,

Coiled round its roots, giving slime for all moisture,
and poison for dew.

Now I but mourn o'er a grace unrenewed. All in
vain do his kisses

Press on a passionless cheek, that is cold as the
conscience I slew.

4

One supreme moment ; no more.   And the joy of it
    died with the using :
One sublime bound to the copestone of bliss, then
    the chilling recall :
One sudden sense of a crown, then the sting of the
    thorns of accusing :
One sudden draught of the nectar, that turned as
    I drank into gall.

5

What shall I curse?   The poor hands that lie life-
    lessly lax when he takes them
    Into his own?   Or the arms that are flaccid and
        powerless to cling ?
Or the set lips without fervour?   The eyes whose
    effulgence forsakes them ?
    Or the thin, quavering, passionless voice that
        refuses to sing?

6

There is no good thing, I think, 'neath the sun.   And
yet somehow it seems to me,
When I saw *her*, that true happiness shone like the
sun from her face
As he drew near to her.   Glimpses of Hyacinth
come in my dreams to me,
Radiant, elated, and clothed with joy as an
angel of grace.

7

All for young Raymond—my Raymond too !   But
there's a curse on my loving ;
Curse of an inward recoiling, and curse of an
outward decline ;
Curse of an outward supineness, and curse of an
inward reproving ;
Cursed most of all in that memory of intercourse
other than mine !

8

What shall the end be?   Ah me, my wrecked reason
refuseth conclusions.

Lacks there but madness to fill up my cup of
reproach to the brim?

God! send me rather the sharp fires of hell than the
reign of delusions!

This is the one thing I ask thee, to slay me ere
judgment grow dim!

V.

WHY walk we softly and whisper to-day, as if one
in a fever

Slept, and life lay in the stifling of sound, and the
batement of breath?

Know we not well that no step can awake her, no
dissonance grieve her?

Know we not well the omnipotence of the last
febrifuge—Death?

2

Surely we know she is dead to our reverence and
          muffled dissembling,
     Past all our little proprieties, in unprofanable
          spheres ;
Yet we walk softly, and whisper, and do our least
     !   office with trembling,
     As if the vibrating air yet made converse of sound
          in her ears.

3

This is the riddle of Death : while she lived, no such
          reverent seeming
     Silkened our ways.   She is dead, and we whisper,
          move softly, and weep ;
As if our delicate walking would rhyme with the
          peace of her dreaming,
     As if the music of whispers would deepen the hush
          of her sleep.

4

Surely we know all must die : yet we cherish and
hoard up our reverence,

Until the known are unknown ; then subside to
unechoing feet.

Were it not wiser and better to count on the moment
of severance,

And pay the dues of the tomb in the house, in the
mart, in the street ?

VI

HYACINTH'S mother. . . . One question appals
  me. When spirits are bounded
No more by strait circumscription and narrow
  availment of brain,
When they are done with all mediums wherewith
  our dull nature is rounded,
Can they then look, soul to soul, on the secrets
  of such as remain?

2

Then she knows all; and my heart like a scroll lieth
  open before her,
  And I am read as I am in the merciless noonlight
    of truth,
As the high-priestess of craft, the arch-scorner, the
    self-god adorer,
  As the contemner of innocence, and the deceiver
    of youth!

3

Hush! This is dotage of morbid timidity, fruit of
    long waking,
  Offspring of death-bed anxieties, weak suicidal
    despair.
I will throw off superstition, arise when the daylight
    is breaking,
  Look on the body, and touch it, and breathe in
    the death-laden air.

4

I will be friendly with death, and familiarly handle
    and think of it,

Call its deep peace a delight, and its etiolation
    a grace.

Surely 'tis wise now and then just to sip at the cup
    ere we drink of it,

Wise to strip Doom of its terror by looking it full
    in the face.

VII.

L O, where it lies, not yet wholly cut off from the
    land of the living.
What is there in it should haunt me, and thrill
    with mysterious awe?
Is it not matter as I am, obedient to sunlight, and
    giving
Even in its shadow the tenebrous token of natural
    law?

2

Yea, by the shadow it casts one might reckon the
hour of the morning.

It is then subject of time, and the changing
relations of space.

Is it then other than I, save the fashion of outward
adorning,

Other than I, save the shroud, and the flowers, and
the hue of the face ?

3

Oh, who will read me this Death !   Who will read me
this stranger Life-mystery,

Pierce to its primary subtlety, seize it, and drag it
to light,

Show me its essence, its fount, its transmission, its
law, and its history !

Oh who will teach me what Day is, ere yet I go
down unto Night !

4

Ever the problem besets me, in labour, in sorrow, in
    laughter :

Mystery of mysteries, too wide for conception, too
    deep and too high !

Imbecile ! What doth it profit to gaze on the mists
    of Hereafter !

Turn me away from them. Eat, drink, be merry,
    To-morrow we die !

VIII.

AH, but to-morrow we die not. For morrow, and
morrow on morrow,

Each with a cry of awakening, and stretching
importunate hands,

Rending the garments of sleep, and unveiling new
danger and sorrow,

Bursts on the soul of the schemer, and bids it take
heed how it stands.

2

Hyacinth cometh.   No delegate Fury of wrath
    unrelenting
  Ever tracked mortal as tracks me the pallid
    reproach of her face.
Yet even one tear is denied me.   I find me no place
    for repenting,
  Cast forth all lawless and lonesome beyond the
    attraction of grace.

3

Oh, there are deep and dark places on earth where I
    fain would be lying,
  Fain would be sleeping unrecked of, and hidden
    away from the sun,
Where is no next, and no imminent, where even
    death is past dying,
  Where is no doing or undoing, where all is done
    and undone !

4

What have I done that the heaven frowneth o'er me,
     and earth reeleth under !

  Hypocrite heaven, and hypocrite earth, as if sin
       were yet young,

And it behoved you to trumpet the marvel with
   .¦   tempest and thunder !

  Ye who have smiled upon sin since the song of
       Creation was sung !

5

Have ye not smiled upon all the seven sins, yea, on
       seventy times seven,

  That ye must blare out your wrath at *my* deeds
       with tempestuous din ?

Were ye not glowing in greenness, oh earth, and in
       azure, oh heaven,

  When the fair hand of our mother was laid on the
       key-note of sin ?

6

Was your complaining thus thunderous, the hue of
your vesture thus sable,

When the fell Serpent hissed hideous triumph with
pestilent breath ?

Were ye so fruitful of gloom when the life-blood of
innocent Abel

Wrote on the flowers of the field the first line of
the annals of death ?

7

Where were your flood-gates of anger when Ammon
encompassed Uriah,

Victim of lust, in the fore-front of battle fell prone
to the earth ?

Hid ye your beauty with sackcloth and weeping when
Queen Athaliah

Spared not the innocent souls whose one crime was
the fount of their birth ?

8

Can I not picture you glorious in verdure, and azure,
     and amber,
  When the proud Tullia swerved not her wheels
     from the corse of her sire?
Can I not conjure the sunshine that gilded the
     porphyry chamber,
  When the blind son of Irene lay moaning his
     eyelids of fire?

9

Ha, ye must flash! ye must bellow!   Yet have ye no
     potence to scare me.
  Full in the face of your fury I tell you my life is
     my own;
And I shall end it to-day, let your thunderous futility
     dare me
  Even as it will.   I am I—I am mine.   God-for-
     saken, alone!

10

Yea, and I know it is sin, and as sin I yet dare it,
and do it.

Death is a light thing, and death is your inmost,
your utmost, your all !

And if the wages of sin is but death, see, I crave it.
I sue it ;

Sue it as wages, for worse thing than life is can
never befall.

11

Oh for the Sea !   'Twere so easy to cease in its
yielding embracement,

Caught like a rain-drop, and merged in the huge-
ness of infinite rest,

Only the laugh of a ripple o'erbubbling the dimpled
displacement,

Then the great level of calm, and the hush of the
passionless breast.

12

Curse on those undulous pastures, and far-vista'd
    woods unavailing,
  Scant of contiguous umbrage, unmeet for the tomb
    that I crave !
Oh for the dark-curtained sleep of the Sea, for her
    kindly, unfailing
  End of all dolorous things in the bliss of the kiss
    of the wave !

13

Would that my oft-haunted river were deep as the
    concave of ocean,
  Tideless as Pontus, and true to the secrets of
    final despair !
God ! it would wake me, methinks, to be dragged
    in its libertine motion ;
  Stranded, perchance, to be flouted once more by
    the sun and the air.

14

I do remember that once in my wanderings I noted

a lakelet,

Strangely sequestered, and high on a ridge un-

frequented and steep.

Green things lapped lovingly of it, and lightly in

many a flakelet

Floated shed tribute of lilies thereon, a sweet

refuge—and deep.

15

Thither I'll hie me, and lay down my burden of sin

and of sorrow;

Cast me therein with one instant and ultimate

thrill of release;

And the great world shall go round to renewing of

days; but to-morrow

I shall be deep in the heart of the hills, at the

centre of peace!

PART THIRD.

I.

IT was a fever, they tell me: to me 'twas a sleep
and a waking;

Yet not a sleep without dreams: if indeed they
were dreams that I saw.

Never, I think, shall I call it a dream: but the truth
and the breaking

Up of all dreams, and a glimpse of superlative
being and law.

1

2

Sweet, passing sweet, is this light of the morning, by
green leaves made tender,
Tender and mellowed on lids fever-folded, yet sick
of repose ;
Even as this leaf-mellowed glow to the flood of
meridian splendour,
So is the life that we live to the life that such
visions disclose.

3

Sweet is this dance of the shadows of leaves on my
coverlet, ever
Shifting and changing, yet silent, impalpable, fretting no fold ;
Even as this shadowy dance to the forest's tumultuous
quiver,
So is the life that we live to the life that in vision
is told.

4

As I lie here on the dubious bank betwixt waking and

    slumber,

  Life on earth seems but a window that straitens

    our view of the skies ;

And all our fluttering joys and life's things of desire

    without number

  Are but the lattice-leaves, tempering God's light to

    our infantile eyes.

5

I have beheld what hath changed me, I know not in

    body or spirit,

  Far in a region where leagues are no measure, and

    time is no bound ;

Up in the realms imperturbable, which the high

    spirits inherit ;

  Out of the reach of all seasons ; beyond the last

    echo of sound.

6

First there came one like a storm-cloud, and bore me
high up on a mountain,

Showed me the kingdoms of earth, and the glory
thereof, and the power ;

Ope'd me the well-springs of Love, drew the wine of
Desire from its fountain :

"Bow down and worship," it said, "and all this
will I give for thy dower."

7

Then came, all star-girt, another, and caught me
away, and I know not

Whither he bore me, because of the pure inacces-
sible ray,

Save that it was in the land where the beams of
eternity flow not

From any sun, and no morning or evening divideth
the day.

8

As in a chrysolite sea I beheld the great cycles of
    story,

    Circling and widening afar at each pulse of the
    will of the King:

But where I stood there was darkness that marred
    the immaculate glory;

    Shadowed therein I beheld me, a guilty and shud-
    dering thing.

9

And while I stood all estranged, without welcome, or
    greeting, or token,

    There was a voice in my soul, "Thou must weep,
    if thy spirit would live."

Came a great longing for tears, and the spell of the
    vision was broken,

    And on my bed I lay tremulous, weeping, and
    crying, " Forgive ! "

10

Lo, by my side, all in white! it was Hyacinth, fair
　　　as the morning;
　And on her face were the meekness and peace of
　　　an angel of heaven.
Keener than anger is pity, and love than the weapons
　　　of scorning!
　Lifting her finger, she smote me with—" Hush !
　　　All is known, and forgiven."

II

LITTLE by little the tale of the stroke and the
fever I gather,

As I lie bridging oblivion, and weaving her words
into form ;

How I was found as one dead, on a hill-side, by
Hyacinth's father,

Struck by the uppermost boughs of a tree that was
wrecked in the storm.

2

How, after days of the semblance of death, there
    came fever and raving ;
  How the brain's anarchy loosened the tongue from
    its wonted control ;
How I spoke wildly and darkly of Raymond and
    Hyacinth, craving
  Death for my body because of them, uttermost
    death for my soul.

3

How it was deemed as a duty to one whom no care
    could recover,
  Freely to search for some token of kindred, or
    trace of a friend ;
How in the scrutiny Hyacinth chanced on the words
    of her lover,
  Read and knew all, yet forbore to add woe to my
    imminent end.

4

How, too, at length I had rest, and the burden of
heavy complaining
Changed to the sighing of rapturous vision, and
tranced repose.
Well: it is over.   Where now is the passion that
knew no restraining?
But is the evil past?   Will the shed petals return
to the rose?

5

Full of crushed fragments my hands are.   Ah me, can
I e'er re-unite them
Into the sacrament cup of the love I have broken
and spilt?
How they two clung as the vine and the elm ere I
saw, but to blight them!
Is there a river of tears that can cleanse out the
mildew of guilt?

6

Is there no way?   Ah, no way!   From my raving her
    father, astonished,
  Gathered a part of poor Hyacinth's story, sufficient
    for wrath ;
Led her away from me, questioned her, threatened,
    upbraided, admonished,
  Tyrant and father by turns ; till, unpurposed, their
    devious path

7

Ceased at the grave of her mother.   Which seeing,
    the old man, with weeping,
  Knelt, and made Hyacinth kneel on the verge of
    the flowerless sod :
" Now, by my dead, hear me swear ; by the heart of
    thy mother here sleeping"—
  And he uncovered his head, and uplifted his hands
    unto God.

8

And as he raised them the gleam of the known wedding-ring on his finger,

  Catching his eye as it glittered, gave form to the words of his oath :

"See it," he said ; "it was her's ; and by all the pure
memories that linger

  Round it, I make it the sign and the seal of a covenant for both.

9

"When I shall offer this ring as a sacred and covenant token

  Unto a convict, the choice of thy father : then love where thou wilt.

Can I more fitly say Never? Enough. When my purpose is broken,

  Go thou to Raymond, and make thyself kin to dishonour and guilt."

10

Could he more fitly say Never?   I know him, a
     puritan cleaving
Unto the letter of covenant, a word-clinging Jeph-
     thah in vows.
He will go down to the grave with his vow in his
     right hand, believing
He hath done well by his children, his honour, his
     name, and his house.

!

III.

I AM not done with my shame.   As a garment it
    clingeth around me.
Even as a shroud it doth cover me paralysed,
    swathed in disgrace.
Fast in the folds of obstruction, as one of the dead
    it hath wound me,
Holding me motionless : and as a face-cloth it
    covereth my face.

2

What shall I do with my life, now I live? Could
there be restitution,

Then were there something to live for, a guerdon
to strive for and win.

Is there no hope, and must life be henceforward a
slow dissolution,

Passive and tearful purgation of soul from unspeakable sin?

3

In the old days there was refuge in orisons, vigils, and
fasting,

Cloistered retirement, and matins, and vespers, and
garments of grey ;

Wherein the broken in spirit caught glimpses of joy
everlasting,

Turning their life into night that the night might
inherit the day.

4

Queens, and Kings' daughters, and delicate damsels,
their pride and their beauty

Laid on the altar of Jesus.   I think of such things
and am fain.

Faugh !   It was cowardice all, and the sickly evasion
of duty !

Shame may be turned to a snare, and repentance
made fruitless and vain.

5

I shall not cease to upbraid me.   My burden is fixed.
I will bear it.

Yet must this bondage of shame be unwound that
my soul may respire.

Hid 'neath the vesture, and next to the flesh, as a
chain I will wear it,

As did the monarch of old that was stained with
the blood of his sire.

6

So may I fight as he fought, with the iron memorial
cherished

Under all kingly array, until life was laid gloriously
down :

Also the world holds him kindly, and tearfully tells
how he perished :

His was a crown and a chain; oh, may mine be a
chain and a crown !

IV.

I HAVE made all my confession; the truth, and
the whole, and truth only;

Made it with anguish of spirit, and weeping, and
hiding of face.

But I have justified *him*. So far well. Single-handed
and lonely

I must begone with my burden. My guilt over-
shadows the place.

K

2

Raymond is far from us.   Driven from his peace by
   my fitful demeanour,
   Sudden he leaped at a chance of adventure, and
      passed from his home.
He too must know.   Then my spirit may yield to a
   sorrow serener,
   Seeking some token of duty to beckon me whither
      to roam.

3

Hyacinth fighteth against my new purpose.   His
   love is for ever
   Closed against *her*, so she reasons.   The oath of
      her father endures.
Also she pleads her worth poor; " If in you he has
   found what I never
   Could have been unto him, let the means pass ;
      not the less is he yours."

4

Piteous dove! though thy pardon extend unto
seventy times seven,

  I shall not strain the advantage: thy loving is
better than mine:

Clinging like Sterope unto a mortal, like her I lose
  heaven.

  Now through repentance and duty I look to a
union divine.

5

Surely God loves thee, thou sweet one! The Psyche
that moves in thy moving,

  Looks through thine eyelids, and breathes in thy
breath, is some angel of grace!

Kiss me, oh Hyacinth! that the sweet sense of
forgiving and loving,

  Some little fifth of thy nectar, may pass from thy
lips to my face!

V.

ONCE again out in the breeze and the sun-light,
heaven o'er me, earth under !
Grown unfamiliar by reason of sickness, all
beautiful things
Meet me with hundred-fold welcome, each green leaf
a jubilant wonder,
And the old throb of delight in the music of
fluttering wings.

2

Now I can smile with the flowers; for to-day I have
 learned what hath brought me
Nearer akin to them.   Ere this same summer hath
 numbered its hours,
I shall be mixed with their roots.   There came one
 .'   here to-day who hath taught me
How there is that in my heart which shall lay me
 ere long with the flowers.

3

Science hath uttered its sentence.   I own to a
 transient terror;
Only a little at first, then a sense of unspeakable
 rest.
Taken away from the evil to come!   The long
 bondage of error
Soon shall be over!   I carry my ransom about in
 my breast.

4

Ah, it is well. For I know my own heart : had I
     lived, I had striven
With a too violent haste and much stumbling to
     seize on the prize.
Now I am cast back on mercy, content to be simply
     forgiven,
Beggared of righteousness, pleading but needful-
     ness, Magdalen-wise.

5

Yet it is strange I should smile with the flowers. I
     was wont to dissever
Nature and Grace. Behold Grace lends to Nature
     a kindlier charm.
All things are bright with a glorious light of redemp-
     tion, and never
Seemed all the verdurous umbrage so gracious, the
     rose-blush so warm !

6

Once on a time, to me beauty seemed only a beautiful
 dying,
 Like to the moribund glow of the doomed one,
  illusive as sweet.
Death! I had deemed it the end of all beauty, the
 ⸗ hid underlying
 Worm at the root of all loveliness, making each
  grace a deceit.

7

This from afar. But now, nearer, I hail it the needful
 condition
 Of the superlative life; not a pause, but a step,
  and a birth;
As but a yew-shadowed avenue leading to splendid
 fruition,
 And the fulfilment of that which is writ on the
  flowers of the earth.

8

It is but closing the eye for repose, ere we wake to
the wonder

    Waiting our vision through slumber made strong
to behold the Divine.

It is but turning the web we have seen as yet only
from under,

    That we may look on the tissues of life in com-
pleted design.

9

'Tis but the fall of the seed when the season of
blossom is over,

    Dying to spring up anew from the womb of its
burial clod.

'Tis but the clasp of the die on the coin, which the
mould must once cover,

    Ere it shine forth with the bright superscription
and image of God.

10

Once in mine agony, once in my darkness of purpose
    I sought it,
Wilfully blind to its issues, and caring for respite
    alone;
Trampling the jewel of life under foot that was His
   .ſ   who hath bought it;
Lord, re-unite the poor fragments, and set them
    at last with Thine own!

11

Not with Thine amethysts, not with the emerald,
    sapphire, and ligure,
Lest I be shamed into nought, as a star when the
    sun is on high;
Not with the Urim and Thummim, of Light and
    Perfection the figure,
For I am dark and imperfect; no gem of Thine
    worthless as I.

12

Oh, if it be that a pearl is a tear, as a pearl do Thou
set me

  Where infant-angels shall point to me, asking the
meaning of pain.

So in the day when Thou gatherest Thy jewels Thou
wilt not forget me,

  Though I be dim with remembrance, and shades
of old sorrow remain.

VI.

STRANGELY I wake to high thoughts, and
beneath them a quiet gratulation,
Like a hid brook whisper-quiring the lordly old
music of pines ;
And, around all, as a glory, an incense of sweet
consecration
Wraps me in mists of devotion that soars beyond
visible signs.

2

Through the thin wall that divides us I hear the low
    breath of the sleeper,
All whose blest dreaming is worship, whose veriest
    breathing is prayer.
Oh to be like her! so meet for the Master, so ripe
    for the Reaper,
Clothed on with gentleness, full of sweet amnesties,
    stainlessly fair.

3

Let me but look on her. 'Twill be a sacred and
    privileged portal
Unto new day, but to mark how the stages of
    crimsoning morn
Quicken the life in her cheek—how the mortal that
    shrines the immortal
Grows out of darkness from grace unto grace,
    re-illumined, re-born.

4

Peace to this chamber. Now kneeling I gather the
    breath of her purity.
  See how the delicate pinions of dawning seem
    fondly to sweep
Over faint outlines and twilight suggestions of
    .'   shapely obscurity,
  Brushing the tokens of night from the maiden
    white marvel of sleep.

5

Seems as Aurora were groping for beauty, and, lo !
    having found it,
  Flushes with roseate rapture, and, bounteous,
    hastes to unfold
All the rare gifts she hath gathered from orient, and
    lavish around it
  Various profusion of homage in amber, and crim-
    son, and gold.

6

Not on the mountain-tops only the glad things of
dawning are treasured,

Not in the vaporous magic with bright dreams
bewitching the air,

Not by proud eminence only the scope of her bounty
is measured ;

Sweetest it lies on my sweet, on her face, and her
aureoled hair.

7

Soft sits the light on her beautiful brow ; no such
radiance is given,

In the morn's kiss, unto uppermost leafage or
easternmost peak :

There is no hue on the rainbow-winged messengers
floating in heaven,

Like the ethereal pigments that blend in the bloom
of her cheek.

8

What are thy visions, fair slumbering sister? What
        alchemy hidden
    Orbeth the tremulous dream-drop that pearls the
        dark fringe of thine eye?
Oh, if thou sorrowest even in sleep, by thy sleep am
        I chidden:
    There was no tear in the peace of thy dawn ere my
        shadow passed by.

9

I should go from thee; from all that is thine; and
        yet fondly I linger,
    Thinking some providence yet may redeem the
        foul wrong that I weep.
May not some juncture of good, like an angel with
        beckoning finger,
    Wave me the way of redress, and establish thy joy
        ere I sleep?

10

Oft where the clouds gather darkest, the star of our
comfort is shining.
Black though the night of our sorrow, who knows
but the dawn may be nigh?
I will not speak of my secret of death, till the signs of
declining
Warn me to flee to the city : to choose me a home
where to die.

PART FOURTH.

L

I.

" I HAVE no heart and no time to go forth to the
world, there to choose me
One who may be to my children a mother in
room of the dead.
Soil-rooted, I am no more of society. I should but
lose me
In its mad vortex. And yet, it behoves me to
choose, and to wed.

2

"No more for love.   As thou seest, I am old, and
my summer is over.

Yet 'tis for love, too, the love of a father who fears
for his own.

It is for them.   Mark, I plead not in guise of a
passionate lover.

Plain in my speech, what I offer are honour and
duty alone.

3

"Beauteous I see thee; yet 'tis not thy beauty that
tempts me to sue thee :

'Tis that I've noted thee faithful in many things,
weighty and small.

Gifted I know thee; yet not thy attainments could
tempt me to woo thee :

Nought I behold save that *thou* lovest *them*, and
they thee—this is all.

4

"If I should say I am rich and thou poor, this were
　　little to claim thee.

　If not for love of my little ones, let my poor quest
　　be as nought.

Cast it aside as unseemly, incongruous : I shall not
　　blame thee.

　Better my children left motherless than a false
　　motherhood *bought*.

5

"Ponder it.　Give me thine answer in peace.　Be it
　　joyous or grievous,

　Thou hast my blessing : thy will shall be sacred as
　　heaven's decree.

If thou rebukest my haste, 'tis because thou art
　　purposed to leave us,

　Therefore I speak ere thou goest ; and what are
　　the world's ways to me ?"

II

" THOU then declinest to answer me openly, till
thou hast pleaded

(Well, too, thou pleadest) the cause of my child.
Would my will were my power !

Mightier things than all words for the same have in
vain interceded—

Her dim sad eyes, and the cheeks that are blanch-
ing from hour unto hour.

2

" But, from my youth up, my word has been sacred.

The roots of mine honour

Must be uptorn ere I yield to the breaking of

covenant vow.

Yet my heart weeps for my darling, yea, bleeds to

have mercy upon her !

And I have pleaded with heaven that a way might

be shown, even as thou.

3

" Yea, were the brand of the law on *thy* name—

shall the mere words offend thee ?--

As I have done, even thus would I do, for the

love of my child.

Couldst thou but show me a way, it were token that

heaven did send thee

That my pledged faith and her heart-wish should

meet and embrace—reconciled."

III.

DOTH the excess of joy kill? When the chalice
of pleasure o'erfloweth,
Is it the time of the end? I am sick unto
death of delight.
Why should I tarry when life is fulfilled, and no
longer bestoweth
Anything better than that which hath been. Let
me sleep. It is night.

2

No sleep for joy! When he brought them together,
        and blessed them in union,
   There was a note in my heart that rang death.
        As I write, once again
Quivers the welcome vibration that rings in the
   ʿ   heavenly communion.
   Oh Thou that comest, come quickly, triumphant
        o'er death and o'er pain !

3

'Tis but the heart of my flesh that doth flutter.
        Thine infinite merit
   Helpeth me mightily o'er the dark mountains that
        Thou too hast trod.
Into Thy hands I commend me, eternal and merciful
        Spirit.
   Come Euthanasia ! Let it be kneeling. . . . My
        Lord and my God !